OK BOOMER

IT'S NOT AN AGE. IT'S AN ATTITUDE

BOOMER ALWAYS COMPLAINS AT THE STORE

WHEN YESTERDAY'S SPECIAL ISN'T AVAILABLE ANYMORE

BOOMER GIVES UNSOLICITED ADVICE

BOOMER DEMANDS YOUR SUPERVISOR

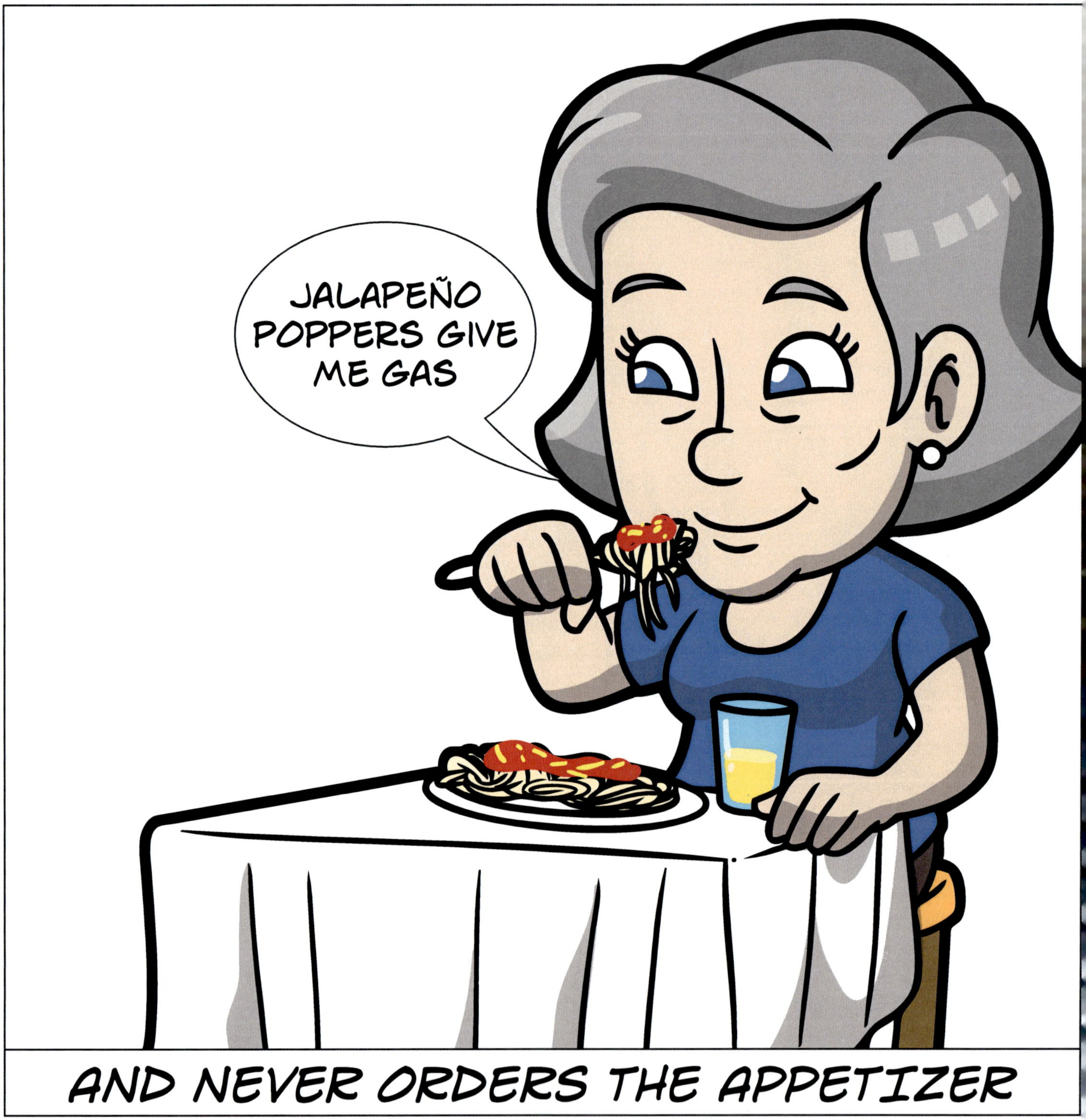

AND NEVER ORDERS THE APPETIZER

BOOMER TRAVELS ALL THE TIME

AND STILL MAINTAINS A LANDLINE

GLOBAL WARMING IS BULLSHIT. IT'S FREEZING OUT HERE!

BOOMER DENIES CLIMATE CHANGE

AND ALWAYS GOES TO THE DRIVING RANGE

BOOMER MAINTAINS A PERFECT LAWN

TO HELP FORGET THE CHILDREN HAVE GONE

BOOMER UNKNOWINGLY MAKES RACIAL SLURS

AND DOESN'T BELIEVE IN ENTREPRENEURS

BOOMER WANTS TO TELL YOU SHE'S BROKE

THAT GUYS FACE IS SLIPPING

AND RECOGNIZES THE SIGNS OF A STROKE

BOOMER STILL READS THE MORNING PAPER

AND PROTESTS AGAINST NEW SKYSCRAPERS

BOOMER ALWAYS TRIMS HIS HEDGES

AGAINST BLACK PEOPLE, SHE ALWAYS ALLEGES

If you want to reach me.

TW: @bradgosse
IG: @bradgosse
FB: @bradgosse
TIKTOK: @bradgosse

If you want clipart from this book.
@vectortoons
VectorToons.com

THE END. WRITTEN BY BRAD GOSSE

FURIOUS GEORGE
NEEDS A SMOKE TO CALM THE FUCK DOWN

WHO the RA
STREETWALKER

CHECK OUT MY OTHER BOOKS AVAILABLE SOON

DADS SECRET FAMILY
MEET YOUR NEW HALF SIBLINGS AND SISTER MOM

BRAD GOSSE

JEFFERY'S ISLAND
THE PRINCE, THE PRESIDENT AND THE PLANE

BRAD GOSSE

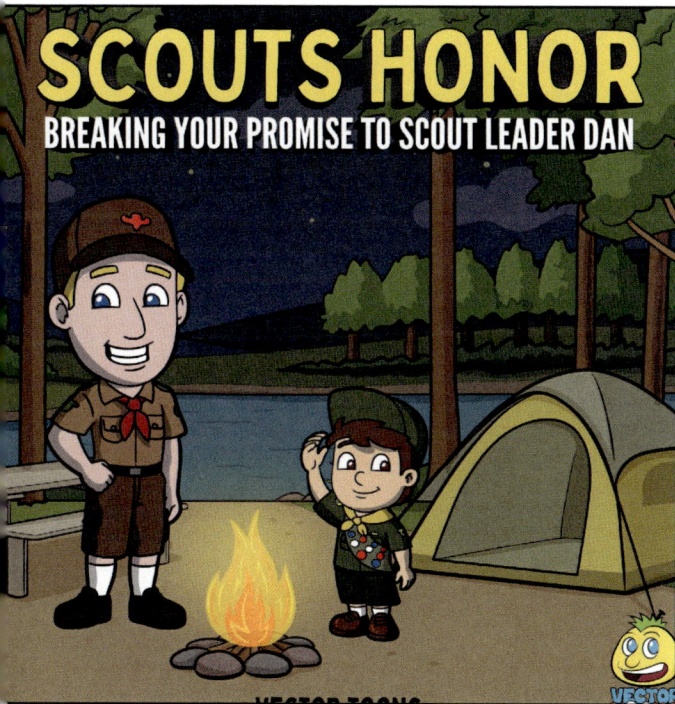

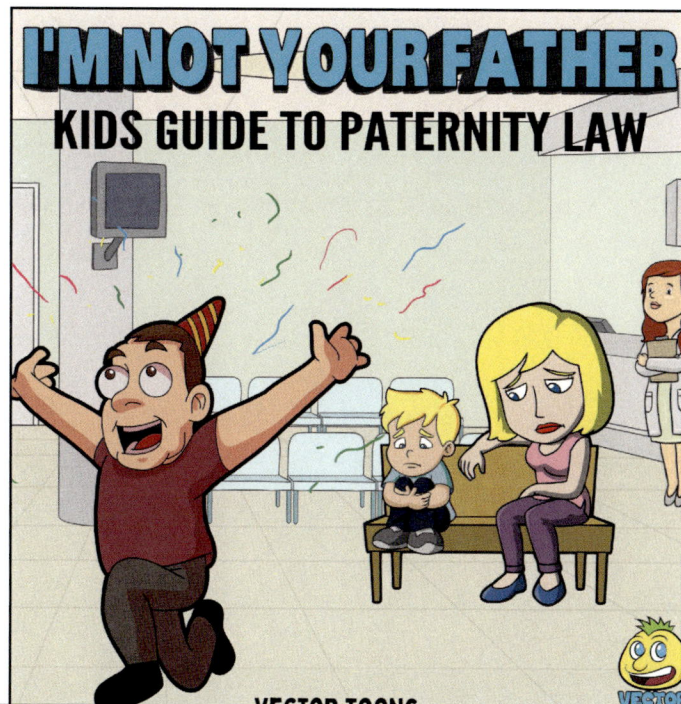

CHECK OUT MY OTHER BOOKS AVAILABLE SOON

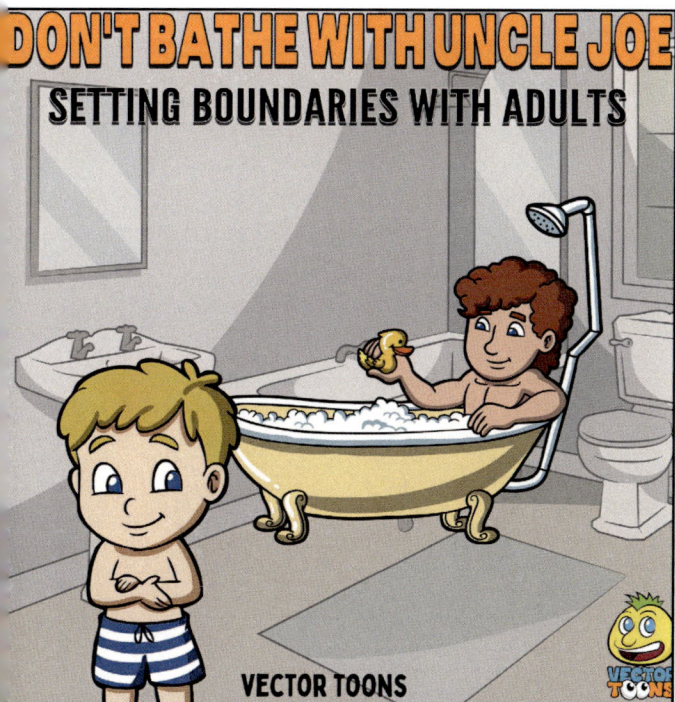

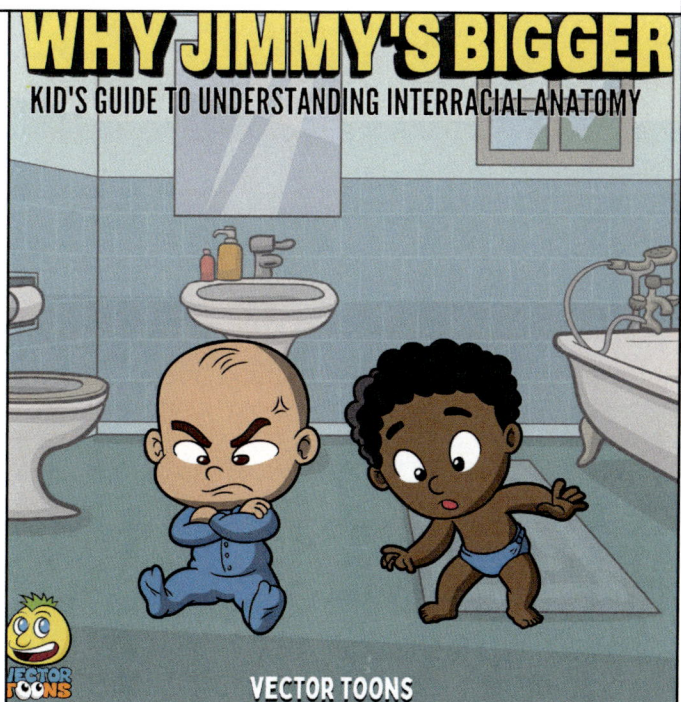

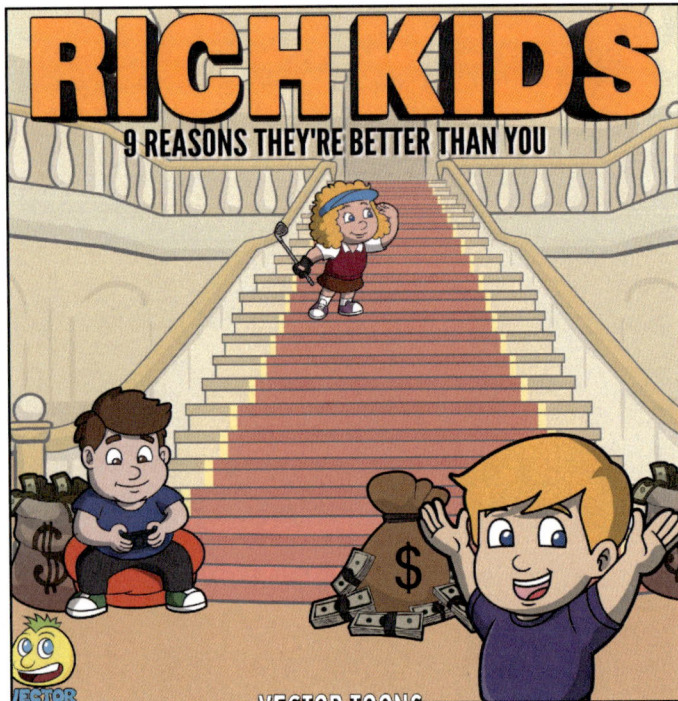

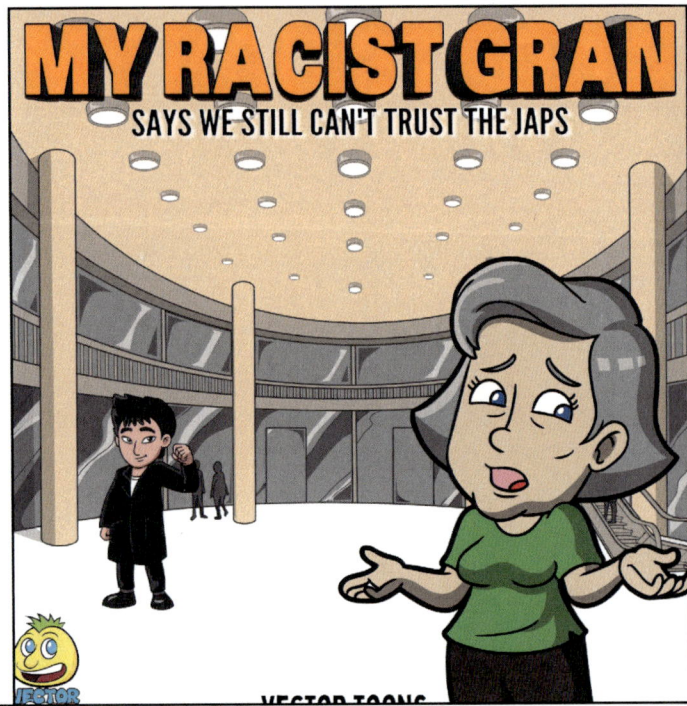

CHECK OUT MY OTHER BOOKS AVAILABLE SOON

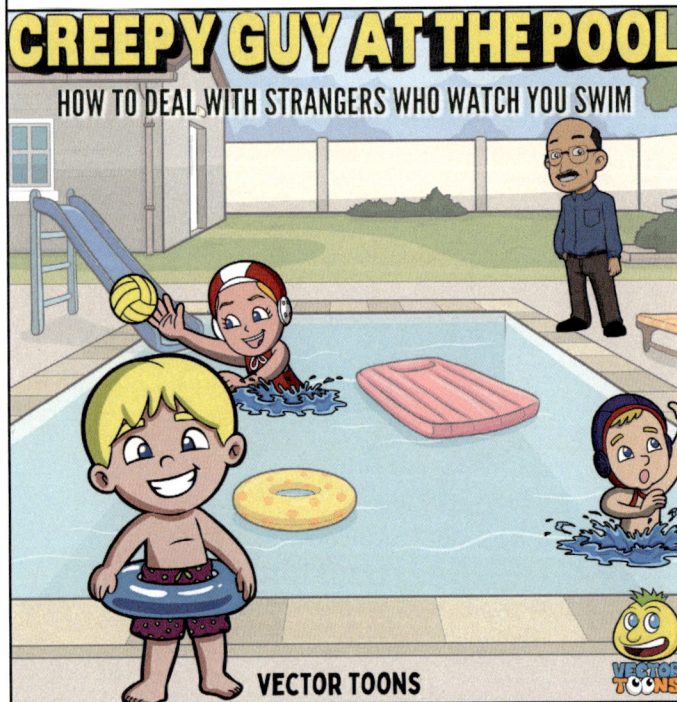

DON`T TALK
UNLESS YOU WANT TO GET DAD INTO TROUBLE

WHEN MOM DRUNK DIALS
HOW TO BEHAVE WHEN STRANGERS COME OVER

CHECK OUT MY OTHER BOOKS AVAILABLE SOON

GROGGY GOAT
SHITS THE BED

BRAD GOSSE

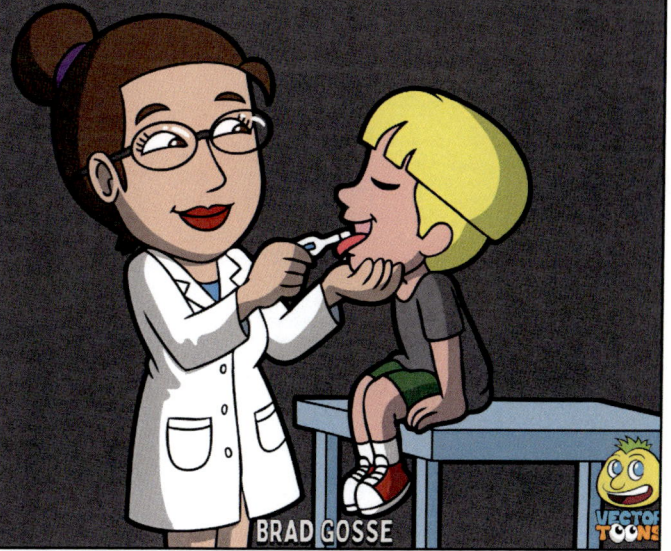

MOUTH HERPES
AND 7 OTHER SIDE EFFECTS OF FAMILY CHRISTMAS SLEEPOVERS

BRAD GOSSE

BAA BAA BLACK SHEEP
DEALS WITH ANOTHER "ROUTINE" STOP

MOM MAKES ME LIE
CONFESSIONS OF AN OVERUSED PINOCCHIO

CHECK OUT MY STICKERS, CARDS AND SHIRTS
BRADGOSSE.REDBUBBLE.COM

I WANT TO
GROW OLD WITH YOU

BI-CURIOUS GEORGE
DISCOVERS SAME SEX PORNOGRAPHY

Made in the USA
Las Vegas, NV
09 May 2024

89703020R00019